Created & Story by Gavin, Mark, & Megan Mariano

Art by Mark Mariano

Edited by Laryssa Wirstiuk

Extra Moo to Gregg Schigiel

www.MarianoBros.com
Brothers Since 1980
New Jersey

MARIANO BROS.

LOUD COW

Loud Cow sat in the middle of the road. She was not happy. Cars and trucks beeped and honked.

"Get out of the way!" yelled a garbage man. "Move it, cow!" shouted a business woman.

Do you know why she's named Loud Cow?

That's why
she's called
Loud Cow.

The road was a mess.
Cats and dogs came to help.

The cats meowed.
The dogs barked.

Can you guess
what Loud Cow did?

Loud Cow mooed.
Her moo was really
loud. Her moo was so
loud she made it rain
cats and dogs.

Up in the clouds,
Natasha Dragon was
taking a nap.

Can you guess
what woke her?

If you guessed
Loud Cow's moo, you're
half right. A bulldog
named Chudley fell on
Natasha's head.

Loud Cow heard a WHOOOSHHH in the sky.

What made that sound?

Loud Cow's moo
sent Natasha
flying to the
moon.

Natasha
liked the moon.
It was quiet.

"Finally a nice place to
nap," she said, as she
curled up to rest.

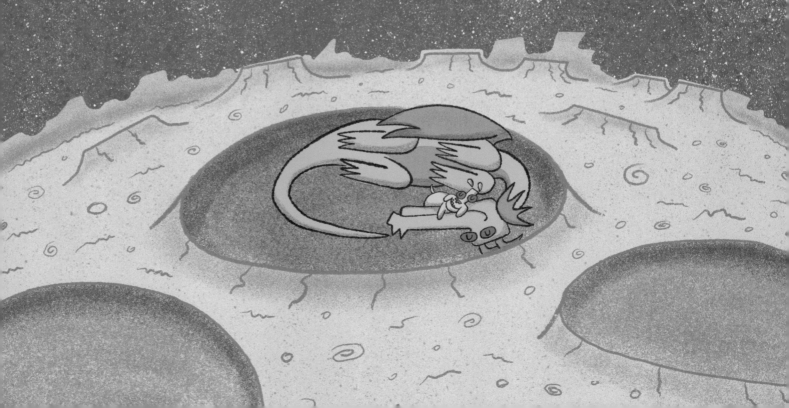

Back home, Pinky Cow rolled up. She was Loud Cow's sister. "What's going on?" Pinky asked. "Where is Quiet Cow?" Quiet Cow was the third sister. They were going to celebrate her birthday today.

"We have a
problem!"
bellowed
Loud Cow.

"We were here waiting for you," said Loud Cow. "Then a pyramid spaceship came down. It beamed up Quiet Cow! I've been calling for you since then."

"That's why you were mooing?" asked Pinky. "Next time use your phone," she said, looking around at all the moo damage. "It's less messy."

Pinky could tell her sister was about to moo again in anger. "Save your moo, sis. We're gonna need it if we drive to the moon."

Loud Cow used her moo to give Pinky's car extra power.

Have you ever seen a moo power funnel?

No? Me either.

With a boom,
they flew. Loud
Cow's moo fuel
zoomed them to
the moon.

Loud and Pinky
searched for the
Moon Mummies.

Loud Cow didn't
feel like looking
anymore. Guess
what she did.

Good guess.
It worked.

The craters
opened. Moon
Mummies riding
Ma Ma Maps
appeared.

The Cow sisters were surrounded.
"Where's our sister?" Loud Cow
boomed in her loud voice.

"I am Bibbidy, leader of the
Moon Mummies," said Bibbidy, leader of
the Moon Mummies. "Come with us."

"Wow, these Moon Mummies are SOOOO colorful!" Pinky said cheerfully as they followed the Moon Mummies to their pyramid palace.

"I don't know if I trust them," said Loud.

What do you think of these Moon Mummies? Do you trust them?

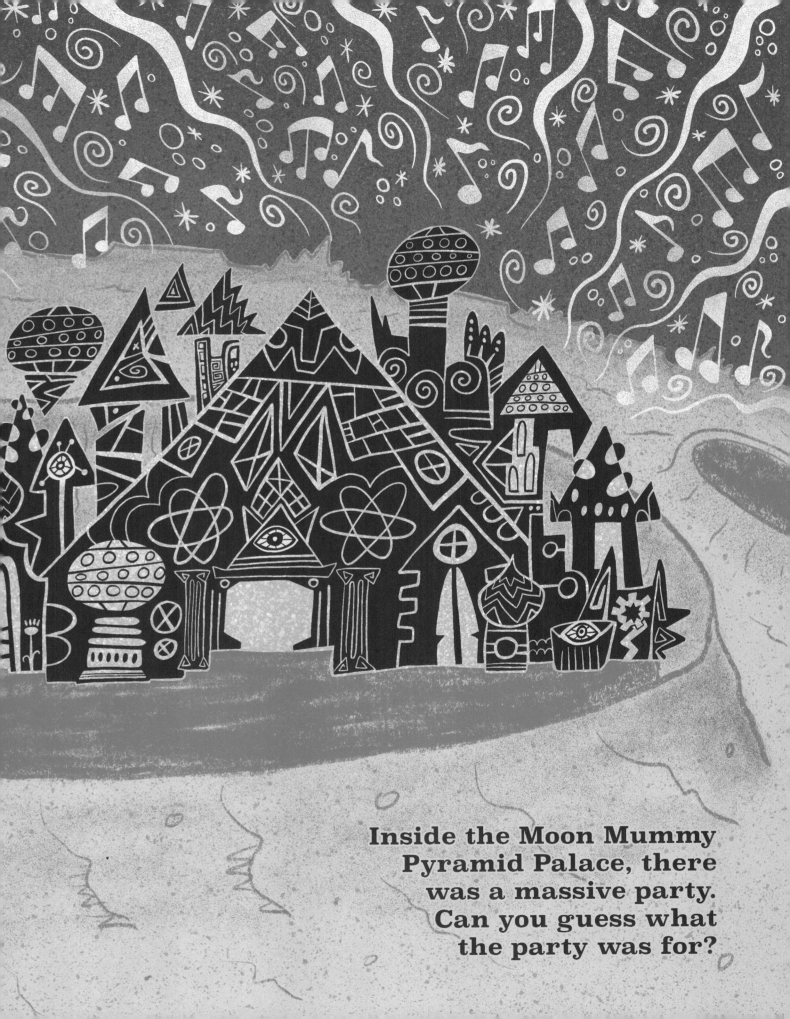

Inside the Moon Mummy
Pyramid Palace, there
was a massive party.
Can you guess what
the party was for?

"QUIET COW!"

the sisters exclaimed.

Quiet Cow greeted her sisters with a big smile, open arms, and open... wings?

Yes, wings. The Moon Mummies gave her wings and a huge party for her birthday.

Quiet Cow greeted her sisters with a big smile, open arms, and open... wings?

Yes, wings. The Moon Mummies gave her wings and a huge party for her birthday.

Loud Cow gave Natasha a big slice of cake. "Join us for the party," she said, "then we'll all have a nice nap. I promise not to wake you up this time."

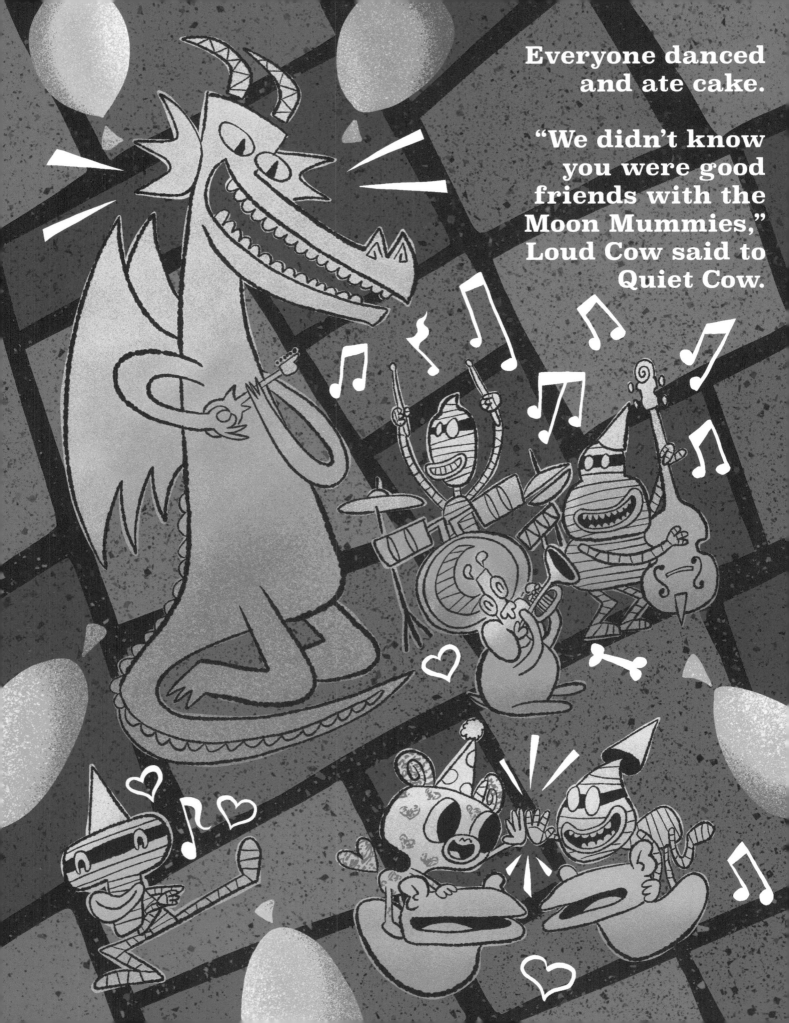

Everyone danced and ate cake.

"We didn't know you were good friends with the Moon Mummies," Loud Cow said to Quiet Cow.

"Really? I've told you many times," Quiet Cow replied quietly. "Maybe you didn't hear me, LOUD COW!"

It was the best party you could ever imagine.

The nap after
the party was
even better.

Other books from the Mariano Family!

**Escape Into Comics:
Laughs and Adventure**

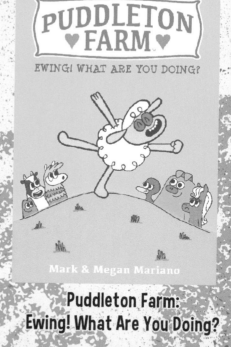

**Puddleton Farm:
Ewing! What Are You Doing?**

Far Out Firehouse

Mundane

Learn more at www.MarianoBros.com

HARDCOVER EDITION, AUGUST 2022
ISBN: 978-0-9823750-4-4

CPSIA information can be obtained
at www.ICGtesting.com
Printed in the USA
JSHW070902180523
41492JS00006B/4